Kimball and the Toy Keeper

By Donna Miller

Illustrated by
David Concidine

Kimball and the Toy Keeper
Text copyright (c) 2009 by Donna Miller
Illustrations copyright (c) 2009 by David Concidine

Published by Do Rae Mi Publishing

Design by David Concidine, Glendora, California
First Printing 2009

ISBN 978-0-9823524-0-3

It was a bright new day. Kimball climbed out of bed without making a sound. He pulled on his Ninja costume, then slid down the banister to surprise Mom who was cooking breakfast.

"Aaah!" screamed Mom. "You surprised me!"

"Are you hungry? Now eat your breakfast so you can be the strongest Ninja around," said Mom.

After breakfast Mom said, "Kimball, go upstairs and get ready for T-ball practice. Don't forget to put your toys away." Kimball rushed to the stairs.

"Kimball, you forgot your sword and Bear," called Mom.

Then Mom glanced out the
kitchen window. In the back yard,
there was a ball, two trucks, and
Tex, Kimball's favorite cowboy.

SOAP

On the way upstairs, Kimball stepped over his pirate boat and some goggles. He also avoided a few scattered army men. Then he remembered what Daddy had said about leaving toys on the stairs.

"Someone could trip on your toys. Now that you are five years old, you are responsible for putting them away."

"What does *responsible* mean anyway?" wondered Kimball. He put on his astronaut costume and launched several missiles and action figures into the corner of his room.

When Mom called him, Kimball flew down the · stairs again, this time dressed as an astronaut.

"Mom, I can't find my *bzmumblemit*," said Kimball under his space helmet.

"We are late! Take off the space suit," Mom said. Kimball stripped off his space suit and left it by the door.

"But Mom," repeated Kimball on the way to the car, "I need to find my baseball mitt for T-ball practice."

"Your mitt should be in the sports box. Did you forget to put it away?" asked Mom.

As they drove down the driveway, Mom pointed to a bat, a flying saucer, and a red bicycle with red handle grips in the front yard.

"You better start putting your toys away or they might get lost."

Kimball did not hear his mother. He was more interested in a rickety old wagon that was being pulled down the street. The wagon appeared to be filled with perfectly good toys. He even thought he saw a baseball mitt among the toys.

"Do you know that guy, Mom? I wonder what that guy is doing with all those toys."

She didn't know.

Later that evening, while Kimball was brushing his teeth, the doorbell rang. He opened the door and found a package with a note that read: "TO KIMBALL."

"Hey, this package is for me! Maybe it's a present from Aunt Dani. It's a phone, my very own phone, and it's ringing!"

"Who was it?" asked Mom. "It was the Toy Keeper," said Kimball. "He says he will take my toys if I don't put them away. Oh, he better not, or I'll use my Ninja moves on him!"

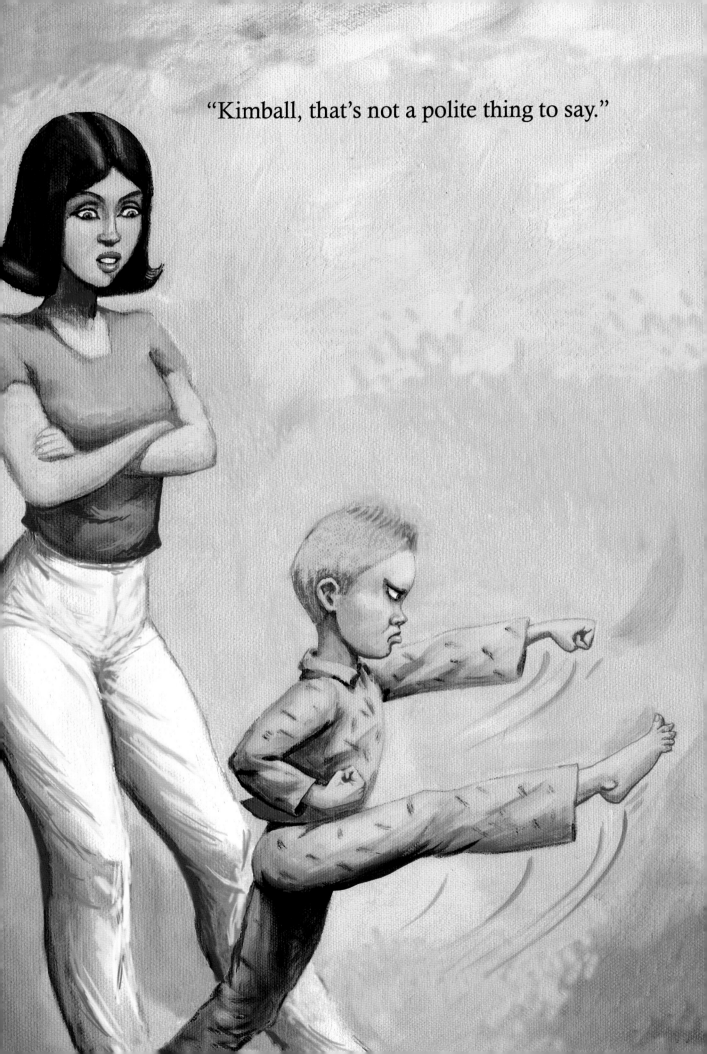

"Kimball, that's not a polite thing to say."

All that night Kimball waited up for the Toy Keeper with his special sword that clanged when he pressed the button. Actually, Kimball waited up only until his eyes could not stay open.

The next morning when Kimball woke up, he looked around and called, "Mom, everything is safe. I protected my toys with my shiny... Mom, where is my sword? Someone took my shiny new sword!"

"Oh no, Kimball. Is it lost? Did you stow your sword in the sword basket last night?" asked Mom. Kimball had not. "Well," Mom reminded him, "toys that don't get put away sometimes get lost."

Then he remembered the phone call from the Toy Keeper:

"I collect toys from girls and from boys.
Put them away at the end of the day,
Or they'll be gone when you want to play."

Later that day the red phone rang again. Kimball nervously picked it up and listened quietly. Then he whispered into the phone, "Yeah, I know, but did you have to take my shiny, new sword that clangs when you press the button? That was my favorite sword... Okay, okay, I will put my toys away."

But that afternoon, Kimball did not straighten his toys. Instead, he spent a long, long time making a complicated booby-trap for the Toy Keeper.

When it was time to go to bed, Kimball was too tired to clean his room, and it was too dark to put away the toys in the yard. He just shoved some of his favorite toys under the bed and hoped he could fool the Toy Keeper.

"Besides," Kimball thought, "I have made the greatest booby-trap in the history of the world. And when I catch that Toy Keeper, he'll be sorry he came to my house!"

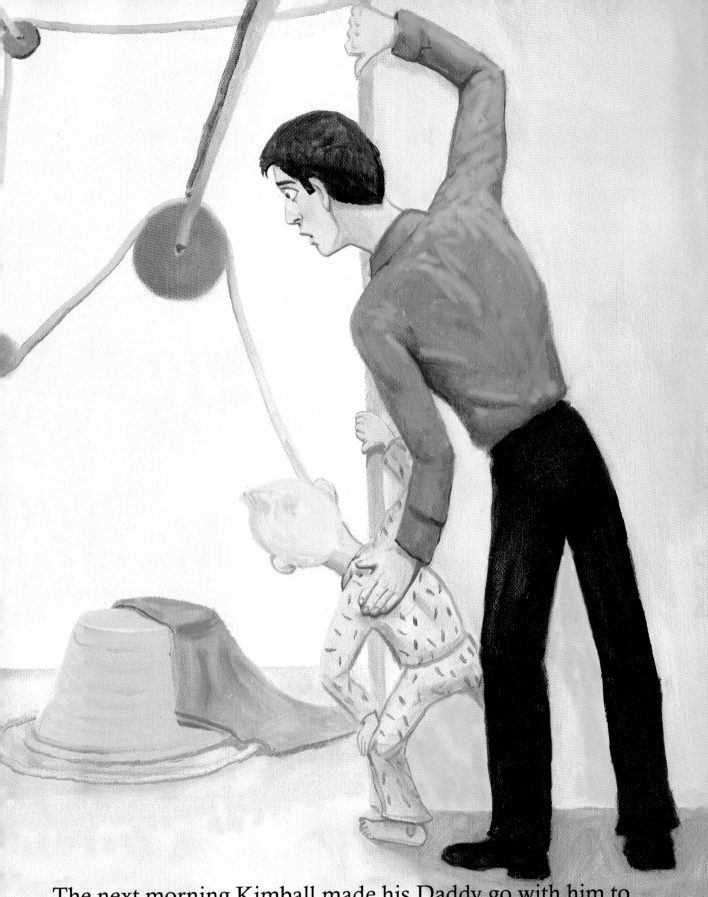

The next morning Kimball made his Daddy go with him to check the trap. They carefully lifted the blanket, but the trap was empty.

"Look out Daddy! Don't step on that lever!" yelled Kimball. "I guess the Toy Keeper saw my trap and was afraid to come in. That will teach him! I bet I don't lose any more toys."

Kimball apologized to his Daddy for trapping him. Then he raced off to his room, hoping with all his might that the Toy Keeper hadn't slipped through the trap to take another toy.

As Kimball surveyed his room, he couldn't see anything missing. But when it was time to go to Jacob's house for a play date, he discovered that his beautiful red bicycle with red handle grips was gone.

"Oh no! Mom, how can I ride my bike next door to Jacob's house? It's not fair! The Toy Keeper should not take my most important toys," whined Kimball.

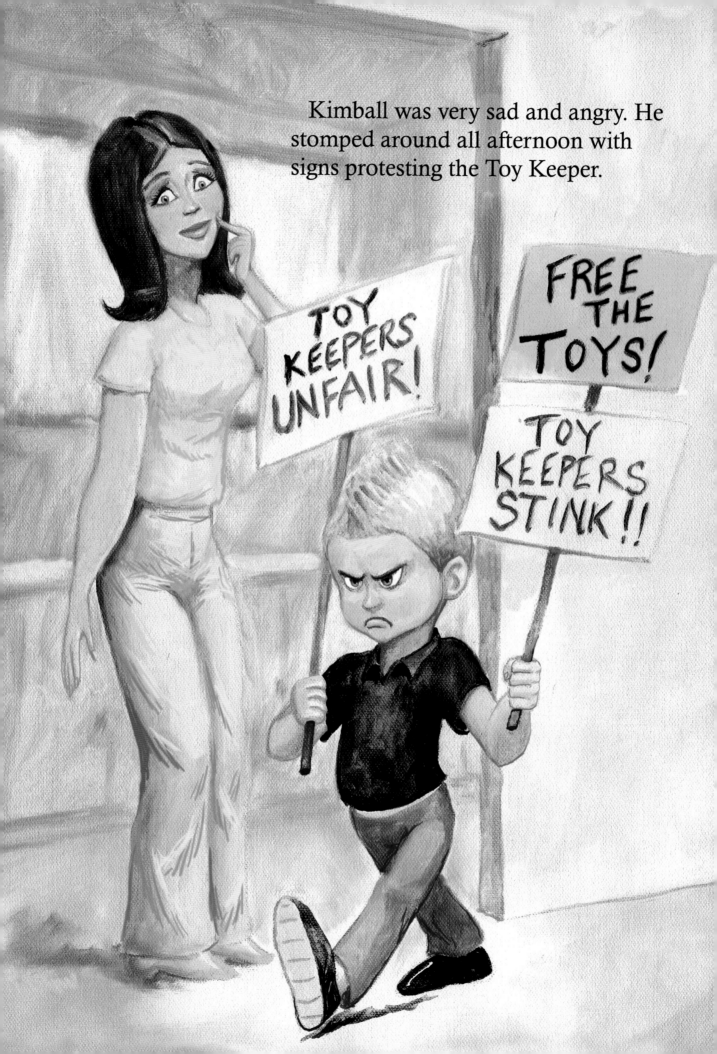

Kimball was very sad and angry. He stomped around all afternoon with signs protesting the Toy Keeper.

Then Kimball dialed the red phone.

"This is Kimball. I have a deal for you, Mr. Toy Keeper. If you will promise not to take my special toys, I will give you a whole box of slightly-used toys that my Mom wants to give to my baby cousins."

"I do not want those baby toys," said the Toy Keeper.
"I collect toys
from girls and from boys.
Put them away
at the end of the day,
Or they'll be gone
when you want to play."

"What did he say this time?" asked Mom.

"He's coming for my Blue Bear. Not my Blue Bear! How will I sleep without him? He's my best friend!"

Kimball thought about his shiny sword that went clang when he pressed the button and his beautiful red bicycle with the red handle grips. Then he looked at his bear and hugged him tightly. Why hadn't he listened to his Mom and Daddy when they told him to pick up his toys?

Suddenly Kimball had an idea. There was only one way to defeat the Toy Keeper. He put on his Super-Kid suit. He adjusted his goggles and began to organize his toys.

"May I help?" asked Mom.

"No thank you. I'm okay. I'm putting my toys away."

Kimball lined his books up according to colors. He put his army men in one box and his knights and kings in another. His costumes fit perfectly into his bottom drawer, and his swords went in their special tall basket.

That night Kimball felt strong and confident. He knew he had out-smarted the Toy Keeper. He shouted, "I will defeat the Toy Keeper forever more by putting away my toys each and every day!"

The Toy Keeper came to Kimball's house only one more time to leave a short note. It read:

You beat me fair and square, Kimball. You outsmarted me and I am returning your silver sword that clangs when you press the button and your beautiful red bicycle with red handle grips. Congratulations.

The Toy Keeper

P.S. Don't forget to warn your sister.

The End.

For my son-in-law, Joel, whose creative mind should not be totally used up on medical science. After all, his "Toy Keeper" would do well to come around more often. And to his son, Kimball, who teaches us whole-hearted love for life.

ORDER FORM
(Please photocopy, fill in and mail.)

Mail to:
 Do Rae Mi Publishing
 PMB 243
 411 E. Huntington Dr. Ste 107
 Arcadia, CA 91006

E-mail: doraemi46@yahoo.com

I wish to purchase_____copies of:

Kimball and the Toy Keeper

Total price, including tax and postage, is $19.95 per copy.

Please send information on Author Readings or Seminars_____

Enclosed please find payment of $_____

Check payable to: Do Rae Mi Publishing.

Send order to:
(Please print legibly)

Name_____

Address_____Apt. #_____

City_____State_____Zip_____

Phone (   )_____

Discounts for multiple book orders (10 or more).

Do Rae Mi Publishing
626 2510365